Faking It for the Boss

A Faking It Series Novelette

Tracy Brody

This novel is entirely a work of fiction. The incidents portrayed in it are the work of the author's imagination. Any resemblance to actual persons, living or dead, events or localities is entirely coincidental, unless you're my friend as I do occasionally, with their permission, name a character after friends as a thank you for their support. So be nice to this author and you can show up in a book.

Faking it for the Boss

ISBN: 978-1-952187-18-6

First Edition

Also available as an ebook

ISBN: 978-1-952187-19-3

Faking It For The Boss
By Tracy Brody

Olivia thought wearing a fake engagement ring to her job interview was a harmless little fib, but when she earns the company's incentive trip, the lie spirals out of control. With no other options, she invites her friend and longtime crush Bash—an Army Green Beret—to pose as her fiancé on the cruise. Sharing a cabin and bed, Olivia's attraction to Bash reignites, despite her mother's warnings about his player reputation. As they attempt to fool her boss and co-workers, Olivia and Bash must confront their feelings and decide if they're truly fooling everyone else, or just fooling themselves.

Chapter One

"The Cruzes are going on a cruise." The security agent joked as she read Bash's name off his passport and checked their documents.

"We're not married yet." Olivia flashed the cubic zirconia ring on her left hand.

"The way he was looking at you, I mistook you for honeymooners." The rep opened Olivia's passport.

"We're going on my company's incentive trip." Olivia drew in a breath and willed her heart to slow down.

"Congratulations on both. If you haven't booked your honeymoon, think about an Alaskan or Mediterranean cruise. When's the big day?"

Never. Olivia didn't answer even though she and Bash had hashed out a backstory in the event they were asked how they'd met, how he'd proposed, and how they'd say they'd begin planning the wedding now that he was back from deployment.

"We haven't set one yet." Bash beamed at Olivia. He was doing a far better job selling them as a couple. "This is our first time going on a cruise. If we enjoy it, we'll do one for our honeymoon, right, sweetheart?"

The agent took pictures for their ID cards and returned their passports. "Wait over there for your security card, which is your room key, ID to get back on the ship in port, and how you pay for any purchases aboard ship."

They stepped aside to wait. Two men in their early thirties joined them.

"Are you with Tarleton Homes?" asked the taller of the pair. Styling gel had his short, light brown hair standing at attention in the front. His blue eyes sparkled with a hint of mischief as he smiled at her.

"I am. I'm Olivia, and this is Sebastián Cruz. He's my fiancé." She hesitated a fraction of a second between the last words, and her stomach constricted at the lie.

"You can call me Bash."

"I'm Jacob. I do flooring acquisitions for the Southern California office. This is my partner, Danny." He introduced the man with receding dark hair and a reserved smile. "The Olivia Novak? Tarleton Homes' rising star?"

"I don't know about that." Her face heated. She'd be the company's falling star if her boss learned she'd misled them at her employment interviews.

"You've been with the company less than six months and cut your division costs enough to earn this trip. That's impressive—and I want to find out how you did that."

"Here you go," an employee handed the foursome their ID cards. "Take the third gangway on the right. Enjoy your cruise."

Outside, the bright sunshine turned to shade as they passed between two massive ships. Olivia breathed a little easier. It shouldn't be hard to dodge her boss on a ship the size of a floating city. Jacob turned and started up a gangway.

"Wait. Is this the right ship?" Olivia froze, and Bash nearly knocked her over.

Jacob turned around. "It's the Regent." He pointed to the name on the front of the ship.

"But it's so . . . small." The ship ahead wasn't even one-fifth the size of the others.

Jacob chuckled and continued up the ramp. "Trust me, it's a good thing. Danny and I went on one of those mega-ships. We had to wait in restaurant lines. We couldn't get two chairs together by the pool, and half the excursions we wanted were booked. With around six hundred guests, we'll get to see you again. I'm sure you want private time with your fiancé, but I want to hear how you were able to cut costs so drastically."

Olivia gave a nervous laugh. Between the other Tarleton employees on their flight from Raleigh to Miami and the shuttle to the port, she planned to board the ship and get some distance from her coworkers and the company's owners. The Regent was not what she'd envisioned.

She'd never gotten the promotional materials about the incentive trip, as it'd gone out months before she joined Tarleton Homes. Technically, she hadn't been eligible for the trip. However, when one of the trip earners abruptly left the company, the owner, Rick Tarleton, insisted Olivia get the slot based on her performance numbers. And, of course, the trip was for two. She couldn't exactly tell him why she didn't want to come.

One lie had led to another. If she hadn't already told people when Bash was due home from deployment, she probably would have lied about that too. Did the lies make her a terrible person? It's not like they were hurting anyone.

She'd wanted her mother to come as her guest, but there hadn't been time for Mom to get a passport. Olivia considered coming alone, though how much fun would that be? Besides, everyone at work expected her to bring her *fiancé*. After she explained to Bash why she'd worn a cubic zirconia ring to interview for the job at Tarleton, he'd agreed to come along and play the role of her fiancé. Why not? The timing worked with him returning from deployment two and a half weeks ago, and he got an all-expenses-paid trip with a long-time friend.

Now, she regretted not inviting a female friend and claiming Bash's deployment got extended rather than involve him. How would she dodge other Tarleton employees and, more importantly, Rick and Eve Tarleton on this small ship?

Her poor judgment in dating a coworker at her prior company put her in this position. Liam seemed like such an upright guy until she discovered the sexts between him and another woman. He turned out to be a player with commitment issues—not unlike her birth father.

Everything about the job opening at Tarleton made her a perfect fit—except for Olivia's coworker warning her that Tarleton's owner was unlikely to hire a single woman because of what happened with the last woman in the position. So, what if she put on a fake engagement ring to interview? It wasn't like she lied about her experience, which made her qualified for the job, and she'd proven she could do the job too. Except she hadn't envisioned that wearing the ring would spin out of control. But she needed Bash's help to sell this lie a little longer if she wanted to keep the job. Then, she would announce their breakup after the trip. Then she'd be done with the lies.

"Wow." Bash surveyed the elegant lobby. "This is way better accommodations than my last six-month working vacation." Bash didn't say where he'd been deployed to. He rarely talked about work. Olivia only knew that he was in the Green

Berets at Fort Liberty because Lola, his grandmother, had told her.

They made their way to their room on the fifth floor—or was it a deck?

"Am I carrying you over the threshold, sweetheart?" Bash flashed that flirtatious smile which countless women fell for.

"That's for a honeymoon, not an engaged couple." And they were neither.

He opened the door and motioned her in first.

Of course, there was only one bed. Small ship. One bed. She was oh-for-two with the cruise gods. *It's okay.* She and Bash were adults. And he knew why he was here. She wouldn't make the mistake of hooking up with her friend. She was over the heartache caused by Liam's betrayal; she wouldn't fall for a player. That type of man wasn't willing to commit or take responsibility for his actions.

Chapter Two

One bed.

Bash stared at it, willing his body not to get ideas. The message wasn't getting from his head to his junk, maybe because his heart wanted more with Olivia than pretending.

Had she told people he was her fake fiancé *because* he was a convenient option with not being around? Or did picking him mean something? That question had crossed his mind dozens of times since she invited him on the cruise. He didn't expect it was because she'd suddenly fallen for him after the ball. Not when flirting with Olivia for nearly a decade had gotten him nowhere.

He set his backpack and her carry-on on the floor rather than the bed. Maybe the couch pulled out. If so, he'd offer to sleep there. It'd be better than the cot he'd slept on for the last six months. "Do you know what excursions the guy you replaced booked?" he asked, looked out the floor-to-ceiling glass door to their private veranda.

"He never responded to my email, but Tarleton's contact person said we can change them onboard."

"Whatever will be fun. Let's go explore the ship." Before he said something stupid regarding sharing a bed.

At the end of the hallway, luggage was lined up in neat rows.

"Should we find ours and take them to our room?" Bash mused.

"I guess so." Olivia started looking for her suitcase.

"Just leave those." Jacob and Danny arrived as they looked for their bags. "They have someone who will take them to your room. And I bet Tarleton has arranged for them to leave us welcome goodies," Jacob added in a low tone. "Where are you two headed?"

"Just checking out the ship." It was ingrained in Bash to know the lay of the land. In this case, the sea. "We have time before the lifeboat drill, don't we?"

"They'll do that shortly before we get out to sea. We're going to the Oceana Room to see if we can move our reservation time back to be there for the sunset."

"Do we need to make reservations for mealtimes?" Olivia asked.

"Not if you want to eat in the regular dining room. Danny and I are foodies. Since the company paid for the cruise, we figured we'd splurge on some upscale dining. What about you?"

"I'm just back from deployment. Anything other than an MRE is good with me."

"You're military?" Danny eyed him warily.

"US Army. Is that a problem?"

"Not for us, it's just the military tends to have a reputation for . . ." Danny struggled to find the right word.

"Being homophobic?"

Danny nodded.

"We've come a long way since before the 'don't ask, don't

tell' days." But he'd learned better than to start listing off his gay friends or his cousin. "Besides, you won't be hitting on my gorgeous fiancée."

"No," Jacob lowered his voice. "But you probably want to watch out for Griffith from the Chicago office. He has quite a reputation. He brought his girlfriend on last year's incentive trip to Napa. He and Courtney—the rep you replaced,"—he said to Olivia—"still hooked up. After the girlfriend caught him leaving Courtney's hotel room, she locked him out of their room while she packed, then left the trip early."

Olivia stiffened under Bash's hold. "Sounds like she dodged a bullet."

"I'll say. He's an ass." Danny said as they stepped into the elevator. He pressed the button for the top floor.

"How did you two meet?" Jacob asked.

"We went to high school together," Olivia answered.

"High school sweethearts? You've been together a long time, then." Jacob glanced at her left hand. "About time you put a ring on it."

"Unfortunately, we never dated in high school," Bash said.

"No?" Jacob raised an eyebrow.

"Was it your junior year when you transferred to Park-side?" he asked her.

"Yes. Bash's girlfriend was the first friend I made there."

"After we broke up, it didn't feel right to start dating my ex's good friend." Then Olivia began dating one of *his* friends. While that hadn't lasted long, Bash had started dating Juliana. He and Olivia had known each other for ten years, but the timing had never worked out for them to date.

"Sometimes fate keeps you apart until the timing is right." Jacob put a romantic spin on things.

Bash had taken Olivia to his last military ball as a friend, hoping it could finally be more. She had just dumped scumbag Liam, and, for once, neither was dating anyone. Things were looking good when he got spun up doing containment after the 82nd Airborne colonel's wife dropped the bomb about the general ordering Colonel Holmstrom to marry—right in front of him, Olivia, and a half dozen other operators. There'd been no fairytale kiss ending for him and Olivia that night. This cruise might be his last chance to take things out of the friend zone.

"Well, I did kiss her at a party after we graduated."

"And what happened?" Jacob leaned in closer.

"She didn't reply to my texts and calls."

"Because I found out you'd made out with another girl in the hot tub *at that same party*."

The look on Olivia's face twisted Bash's gut. He'd hurt her. Not intentionally, but it was there between them. If he had a hot tub time machine, he'd go back and rewind that day. "Not exactly," Bash started.

Jacob made a slashing motion across his throat, but Bash needed to clear this up.

"That was *before* I kissed you. I'd been drinking, and *she* kissed me. Probably to make her ex jealous."

"We'll go check with the hostess about changing our reservations. Catch up with you in just a minute." Danny said. He and Jacob escaped to the hostess stand outside a snazzy restaurant.

"I wanted to take you out before I left for basic training." If he had any idea why she didn't call back, he would have pushed harder and explained then.

"Whatever. We were teenagers. It didn't go further than a few drunken kisses at a party."

"I stopped kissing you because one of the guys opened the door and made the 'nail her' sign. I wasn't going to do that to your reputation," he explained as Jacob and Danny returned.

"And now you're together," Danny said with false brightness in his tone.

Except they weren't together. Not in the real sense of the word.

"Were you able to get your reservation changed?" Olivia diverted.

"Yes, tomorrow night at 7:45. But it had to be a table for four, so you're dining with us."

Bash and Olivia exchanged glances.

"Our treat," Jacob continued. "Consider it an early wedding present."

"You don't have to do that," Olivia said quickly.

"We want to. I'm also going to pick your brain on how you were able to cut costs as much as you did. Clearly, she's not just beautiful, she's brilliant," Jacob said to Bash.

The captain announced the mandatory lifeboat drill over the PA system, followed by a Sailaway party with live music.

"Oh, fun. We love to dance. Let's go." Jacob herded them to the elevator over Olivia's objections. It's not like they could tell them there'd be no wedding to get a gift for.

Chapter Three

Although her plan to avoid coworkers wasn't panning out due to the small ship and Jacob and Danny stuck to her and Bash like Velcro as their cruise buddies, Bash sold the illusion of them being a couple as naturally as he breathed.

After an hour of dancing at the sailaway party, Bash suggested, "Let's see the concierge and check on our excursions before dinner."

"Good idea."

Olivia explained about taking her coworker's spot on the cruise. The concierge searched on her tablet for first Olivia's name, then the former co-worker.

"I don't have any excursions booked under either name. Either he never used his excursion credit, or he canceled because they didn't get transferred. We still have openings on a few excursions in each port." She printed off a sheet and used a black Sharpie to cross through most options for their first port of Cozumel. "You can also book through local companies online or find locals near the dock offering tours and services."

"Good to know. Thanks." Bash handed Olivia the printout.

"I'm sorry," she said. "When I didn't hear back, I should have spent more time checking options so we aren't stuck on the boat doing nothing."

"No worries, we'll find something. Or, with everybody else doing shore excursions, we'll have the pool and shuffle-board courts all to ourselves."

"Thanks for understanding."

"A free trip with my beautiful fiancée. Why would I complain?"

Maybe not being on excursions with people from Tarleton's different offices was a blessing to protect their secret. Since she wouldn't recognize most, she needed to keep her guard up.

She'd worked up an appetite dancing and filled her plate at the dinner buffet.

"You can come back for seconds," Bash teased as they joined Jacob and Danny at a table for eight.

Danny made a face as two other men approached their table.

"You're Jake, right? We met on last year's trip. I'm Griffith from the Chicago office." He set his plate down across the table from Olivia. "This is my golfing buddy, Vance."

"It's Jacob. You didn't bring your girlfriend this year?" His mouth curved into an innocent smile.

"Naw. I'm not seeing any*one* seriously. I wasn't gonna risk drama by picking one over the other." Griffith's gaze roved over Olivia in a way that creeped her out more than if spiders were crawling all over her body.

Pass, dude. You are not. My. Type. She scooted closer to Bash.

Throughout high school, she had crushed on Bash off and

on. Usually, her crushing phase surfaced when he was dating someone. At the graduation party, the alcohol she'd consumed drowned out her mom's advice to steer clear of him. But hearing he'd been kissing another girl not even an hour before he kissed her had gotten him out of her system—mostly.

When Mom caught her crying that night, she'd repeated her warning about Bash being a player. With him leaving for boot camp in a matter of weeks, she hadn't expected a romance to come of a few kisses. Olivia had blown off his texts and calls. What would have happened if she hadn't?

She studied his profile out of the corner of her eye. It only took a second before he must have sensed it and turned to face her. His smile broadened.

"I need to run in the morning to work all this off." Bash patted his stomach. "Are you getting up at 0600 to go with me?"

"I'm on vacation." Olivia shook her head.

"I might see you there." Griffith stared at Bash as if issuing a challenge.

"I'll be on the jogging track. But I won't be setting an alarm since I don't want to wake up my fiancée." Bash played it up.

"What excursions are you doing in Cozumel? We're doing the cooking class and beach escape," Jacob said.

"We don't know yet. There was a mix-up, so we'll probably do something other than the ones offered by the cruise line for tomorrow."

"We booked a parasailing adventure." Griffith exchanged fist bumps with his buddy. "There might be room if you want to come with us."

"Thanks, but we'll pass," Bash beat her to decline the offer.

"Afraid of heights?" Griffith gave a condescending grin.

Bash laughed. "I jump out of planes all the time. Paying to float behind some boat doesn't excite me."

"Are you a skydiving instructor?" Vance asked.

"No. US Army."

"You're a paratrooper?" Griffith took another swig of his drink.

"I have my jump wings."

"But what do you *do* in the Army?" Griffith pushed.

"I'm trained in unconventional warfare, counterterrorism, special reconnaissance, emergency medical, and my specialty is ordnance—dealing with explosives."

"Really? You make it sound like *you're* in Special Forces?"

The way Griffith smirked as he looked Bash over pushed Olivia over the edge. "Bash *is* a Green Beret."

Bash cleared his throat. "Honey, remember, we don't go telling everybody that." He met Griffith's gaze. "It's a security issue. And what is it you do?" His eyes narrowed a bit as Griffith broke eye contact.

"I'm, uh, in sales. And do quite well as evidence by earning the trip again this year." He sat up straighter.

"Impressive. Though I'm more impressed that my fiancée earned it in less than six months on the job." Bash smiled at her.

Griffith's face turned red. Jacob semi-managed to cover his laugh with a cough.

"Are you all going to the onboard show tonight?" Danny, the peacemaker, asked. "It's a 'Rock Through the Ages' tribute."

"Shows aren't my thing. We're going to hit the casino," Griffith immediately answered.

"That sounds fun." She could escape Griffith's suggestive looks, and the show would give her and Bash something to do before they returned to their stateroom with its one bed.

"Let's watch the sunset from the fitness track." Bash placed a hand over hers.

"Sounds great." She hadn't expected the zing of electricity from his hand on hers. They needed people to buy them as an engaged couple, and that meant there'd be touching, likely a few chaste kisses too, but he didn't let go of her hand as they walked to the track and took a spot at the rail, where a crowd gathered to watch the sun slip into the ocean. The sky turned shades of gold and orange.

"Sunsets over the water never get old." Bash brushed his knuckles on her lower back before settling his hand near her hip.

"It is beautiful." And his hand felt good there, even if he was only doing it for show.

"We should get a picture of us with this background." Bash pulled his phone from his pocket.

It seemed like a good idea considering she spotted several couples from Tarleton around, and most people were taking selfies with the sunset. They turned their backs to the ocean. When he slipped an arm around her and leaned his head close to hers, she turned her body into his.

After he snapped some pictures, he angled his face toward her and waited until she met his gaze—nearly forehead to forehead and nose to nose. Her heart beat faster as their mouths moved closer ever so slowly.

Then Bash's forehead crashed into hers.

"Sorry. Didn't see ya there." The man in a Hawaiian print shirt next to Bash apologized, but kept his elbow aimed at Bash's head as he tried to line up his selfie.

Bash guided Olivia away from the rail. "Good thing I didn't drop my camera and have it bounce off the deck. Lola wants daily proof of life photos. I can't send her those when

I'm deployed. Do you want me to send some to your mom too?"

He didn't have her mother's phone number, did he? No, he had to be playing it up for their ruse. "Send them to me. I'll forward some to Mom with an update on our trip." She'd told her mom she was bringing a friend. She just hadn't told her it was Bash. And if her mother saw pictures of her staring into Bash's eyes like she had a minute ago—oh, boy.

THE ROCK TRIBUTE show had been a blast, with a few members of the audience getting pulled onto stage. Thankfully, Olivia and Bash had been near the back, so even though Bash raised his hand to volunteer, the entertainers hadn't ventured that far. If Bash wanted to go on stage, fine, but singing in front of her co-workers was a hard pass for her.

They shuffled out of the auditorium with the crowd.

"Let's go back to the room and look online to see if any available excursions appeal to you. If not, we'll see what's available in port."

"Sounds good." They would have to go to the room and sleep sometime. She wanted to avoid Griffith, and with sharing a room and bed with Bash, it was best to limit her alcohol intake. Drinking always impacted her decision-making.

Back at the room, their suitcases were waiting by the bed.

"Looks like Jacob was right about the gifts." Bash handed Olivia the gift bag from the table.

Inside was a note signed by Rick Tarleton congratulating the trip earners for their achievements.

"What goodies did you get?"

"His-and-her sunglasses." She handed Bash the second

box of designer glasses, then removed hers from the box and put them on. "What do you think?" She turned and struck a pose.

"That my fiancée is smoking hot." He tried his on.

She laughed self-consciously as she removed the sunglasses. "You look very handsome in yours." With his black hair, darker complexion, rich brown eyes, and perfect features, he'd been attractive as a teen. He'd gotten even more appealing as he matured. His broad shoulders tapered to a narrow waist, and the sleeves of his polo shirt fit snugly around his muscular biceps. It wasn't any wonder women succumbed to his flirtatious nature.

He removed the glasses and dug into his backpack. "This is for you." He held out a plastic container. "It's from Lola. She insisted I bring you some *pichi-pichi* she made."

Olivia laughed. "Your grandmother is so sweet."

"Sweet?" he scoffed. "She's got an agenda. She didn't tell me she'd invited you to the welcome home party. But I'm glad she did since you came *and* asked me to be your fake fiancé."

"You didn't tell your family that part, did you?" What would they think of her lie?

"No way." Bash shook his head. "Lola's always liked you. Fake engagement or not, if I'd told her about that, we might come back from the cruise to find she booked the church for our wedding."

Heat crept up Olivia's neck as he casually dismissed the idea of marriage.

He removed his tablet from the backpack. "Instead, I told everyone your mom didn't have her passport, and you felt safer traveling with a friend. One with training, to protect you." He took a seat on the sofa. "What kind of excursions are you interested in? Besides the dolphin swim. I saw how your face lit up when Danny said they were doing that later."

"I would love to do that on one of our stops." She took a seat beside him. "Why don't you pick what you want for this first one? My treat as a thank you for coming."

"I'm the one who owes you for inviting me. I haven't had a vacation like this in, well, ever. Cruz family vacations were usually an extended family reunion with the six of us sharing a room at a budget-friendly hotel. Even trips to the Philippines to see family were nothing like this."

In no time, Bash had navigated to the excursions page.

"Looks like all the dolphin interaction activities are booked. There's the Tequila versus Mezcal seminar and taco pairing and an all-day tour of Mayan ruins. Let me check options not through the cruise line."

After several minutes, he'd booked a private tour offering ATV rides through the jungle and snorkeling. She didn't care that it was a little pricier than a similar one offered by the cruise. It was worth the extra money to keep anyone from Tarleton discovering she and Bash were just friends.

They stayed up another hour booking excursions for the other ports. Bash searched like a man on a mission, checking reviews, scribbling notes on the printout, and managing nearly two dozen open browser tabs. "Yes! We are swimming with dolphins, babe. I'm booking it." He held up a hand for a high five.

Her body temperature shot up. Did he realize he'd called her *babe*? While it didn't sound cheesy coming from him, she knew better than to think it meant anything. He probably used that term with all the women he dated—as in *really* dated. "Well done. You are the man."

"You deserve the best. That's in Costa Maya." He consulted his notes. "We're doing the zip line in Belize, animal sanctuary and snorkeling in Honduras, and once I book this, we're set."

"While you finish up, I'll get ready for bed. Do you, uh, have a side of the bed you prefer?"

"I'm good with either." His head cocked slightly to the side.

"It's a big bed, and we're adults." She got to her feet.

"All right. I trust you not to take advantage of me." Bash winked.

She slipped into the bathroom and closed the door. Between the touching, him calling her babe, and Bash being his most charming self, she needed to cool things down before she climbed under the covers with him.

When she came out dressed in a tank top and shorts PJ set, Bash took a change of clothes into the bathroom. She was under the covers with only the bedside light on when he came out less than five minutes later. Too soon to fake being asleep.

She kept her back to him as Bash turned off the light, then slid in beside her.

"Good night, sweetheart." He made a drawn-out kissing noise.

"Good night, Bash." His humor took the edge off, and as they lay there in silence, she began to relax.

Bash sighed and the bed jostled as he turned. "How did I have the good fortune to be who you picked as your fake fiancé?"

She'd expected, yet dreaded, this question. "You don't want to know."

"Yes. I do."

Fine. It was a fair question. She turned to face him. "I told you how I wore the cubic zirconia ring to my interview. Well, I thought if I didn't wear it when I started work, maybe it wouldn't come up."

"I'm guessing it didn't go down that way."

Not even close. "The first day I had to meet with HR to

do my paperwork, and the woman explained their vacation policy typically requires six months of service first. However, Mr. Tarleton instructed that if I needed time off for my honeymoon before then, it would be granted without pay. I should have said right then that we'd broken the engagement. Instead, I told her the wedding was at least a year away."

"You aren't very good at lying." He chuckled in a way that made her guard slip lower.

"Tell me about it. Mom always said, 'One lie leads to more lies, and it's better to tell the truth.' But this time, I had a valid reason. It was too triggering to face Liam at work every day, and he had no plans on leaving Hanover Tile, so I needed to find a new job." She couldn't risk quitting until she had a comparable one lined up, with Mom being out of work for over four months due to the carpal tunnel surgery recovery taking longer than estimated. "It wasn't fair to not consider me because of my gender or relationship status. While they couldn't ask about my marital status when I interviewed, the ring misled them. But the HR woman found a way to comment that I wasn't wearing the ring. I said it was being resized because I didn't want to risk losing it." Another lie. "Once I got past the ninety-day probationary period and proved I could do the job, I thought it would be safe to end *the engagement* and lying."

"Why didn't you?"

"Because my immediate boss implied the customers wouldn't be comfortable dealing with a single female because of what happened with Courtney. So, I kept wearing the ring. When people asked about my fiancé, I figured saying he was deployed meant they couldn't meet him. I also had pictures of us from the ball to show people. I never expected to earn an incentive trip for two before I could announce my broken engagement."

"I suppose I was going to be the bad guy too."

"They didn't even know you."

"They do now."

Not only that, of course, everyone was falling for his charm. "Maybe you should flirt with the cruise staff."

"I wouldn't do that to you."

"Really? You flirted with me while dating other girls in high school."

"That was a decade ago. I'd like to think I've matured since then. How about we don't talk about breaking up when I've barely become your fiancé."

She couldn't make out his features in the darkness, but his voice held a comforting warmth. "Agreed." Since being with Bash wasn't a hardship, she'd play this out longer. He had matured. However, commitment and faithfulness were also issues of character—which in her experience didn't necessarily change with age. Not for her father. Griffith and Liam were older than Bash and still thinking only of themselves.

Bash was committed to his career—and his family, but she'd seen him extract himself from relationships before they got serious as far back as high school and continuing over the years to recognize a pattern and know they weren't his priority. Just like her mother had never been a priority in her father's life. She'd rather be alone than open herself up to the same possibility.

Chapter Four

WHEN BASH OPENED HIS EYES, the pre-dawn light peeking through the drapes was enough for him to make out Olivia's lashes against her fair skin. A wisp of hair lay across her cheek. He gently brushed the lock aside, wanting to stroke her cheek. Instead, he eased out of bed, careful not to wake her, and slipped on his running shoes. He arrived at the jogging track in time to take in the display of colors before the sun broke the horizon.

A few others arrived at the track before he finished a half hour of running. Still no sign of Griffith, not that it surprised him. Bash hit the gym weights next.

When he returned to the room, he quietly cracked the door open and peeked in. Light filled the room, and he stepped in.

Olivia was already dressed and sat at the desk braiding her hair. They stared at each other for several seconds.

"Sorry that I didn't knock. I thought you might still be asleep. Hope I didn't wake you when I left."

"You didn't. I just got up."

"Did you sleep all right?"

"Yeah. You?"

"Same." Neither were telling the truth based on how long it'd taken for her breathing to convince him she'd fallen asleep. Being in bed next to her had kept him awake, frozen in place longer than he would admit to. "I'm going to shower. Otherwise, you might not sit with me. Do you want to go down and grab a table?"

"I'll wait for you. Unless you want privacy while you get ready."

"Privacy?" He grunted. "Between my siblings and Lola living with us in childhood and my years in the Army, privacy is not something I'm used to. But, if you need privacy at any time, say the word. Give me five minutes, and I'll be ready to go." He retrieved a clean change of clothes and ducked into the bathroom. Usually, he liked to cool down more after a workout, but thinking of Olivia and showering in the same breath meant he needed a cold shower anyway.

Sure, they joked and teased each other over the years, but some invisible barrier went up before things went beyond flirtation. He needed to find a way to disarm that alert warning system. Putting a move on her in a cramped room they shared on a ship where she couldn't escape was not the way to do it. He needed to be patient, stay in the friend's lane, and figure out what approach would convince her his interest was genuine and give him a chance.

When Bash emerged from the bathroom wearing navy cargo shorts and no shirt, Olivia's gaze locked on his bare torso. Heat flooded her face. She'd felt those hard muscles under her hands when they'd danced at the ball, but they were more impressive to the naked eye.

Not that she should be thinking in terms of nakedness. Despite her determination to keep things strictly platonic, the attraction that had always been there continued to build. If there hadn't been the dust-up at the ball, who knows what might have happened between her and Bash later that night if she'd let her defenses down. While Bash had never cheated on a girlfriend—that she knew of—he also hadn't had a long-term relationship since high school. He might blame his job, but seeing all the happily married couples at the ball proved it could be done—if a man wasn't afraid of commitment.

After Bash pulled on a red T-shirt with a flag stencil on the sleeve that fit snuggly around his biceps, he stared back at her. "Is this all right? I wasn't planning to change before we debark."

"Yeah." She got up from the desk. "No need to dress up to ride ATVs on dirt trails through the jungle." She needed to watch her step rather than lead Bash on when he was here as a favor to her. And she couldn't let his six-pack abs and muscled arms cause her to do something stupid.

"The sunrise this morning was amazing. Didn't have my phone to take a picture for you."

"Maybe I'll get up tomorrow morning and peek out our veranda—then get back in bed."

Bash laughed as they exited the room. "Maybe I'll sleep in a little and watch it with you."

Was that innuendo in his voice? A glance at his face only garnered an innocent enough smile.

After the omelet station, they filled plates at the buffet with fresh fruit, meat, and pastries. As they headed toward a table, Rick Tarleton called Olivia's name and waved them over.

"Join us." He motioned to empty seats at his table. "I

heard there was a mix-up, and you didn't get to pre-book any excursions. I'm so sorry."

"No worries. We were able to book an ATV excursion for today. We're zip-lining, going to an animal refuge and snorkeling in Honduras, and my hero even found a dolphin interaction in Costa Maya." She placed a hand on Bash's arm and smiled at him.

"Good. We're visiting the animal sanctuary on our Roatán stop too," Rick said. "But you're still entitled to the same perks as the others. Submit your receipts to the company to be reimbursed."

"That's not necessary."

"Yes, it is. With your experience on the manufacturing side and innovative ideas, you may be the best new-hire decision I ever made."

"You're one of the few women working for us who's earned a trip. What got you interested in construction supply?" Eve Tarleton asked.

Eve's question was the opportunity Olivia had dreamed of. "I worked for a home décor store in college, where I studied business and marketing. One of the sales reps for Hanover Flooring recruited me, and I thought learning the manufacturing end would aid me in what I want to do. Design."

"Oh?" Eve stared intently at Olivia.

"The owner of the décor store had targeted this master-planned community a few miles away. Some of the builders didn't offer much in the way of upgrades other than better quality carpet or flooring. I enjoyed helping our clients pick out tile for backsplashes and paint to make their house an inviting home that fits their personality and taste. When I learned about the opening with Tarleton, I went to the neighborhood you have under construction outside Raleigh. The model home was gorgeous and quite a selling point."

"Thank you." Eve preened.

"I was impressed that Tarleton offered several design packages for their clients. That, alone, makes Tarleton unique and stand out. But, as you know, it takes more than flooring and paint to make a house look like the model home."

"It's a *lot* of work pulling the look together," Eve stated. "Our daughter helps and knows what younger homeowners are looking for. Formal dining and living rooms are out. Home offices are in."

"Right. Few people have an eye for color and design like you do. Most don't know if their style is contemporary, modern, transitional, rustic, or shabby chic. They move their old furniture in and are disappointed that their home doesn't look or feel like the model."

"I have read those comments in reviews," Rick admitted.

"Our quality building along with customization options is why people consider Tarleton higher end than most production competitors, but we can take it up a level." His wife and daughter had a lock on her dream job, but Olivia had planned out a career path that could get her added to their team—if she could sell it.

"What do you have in mind?" Rick leaned forward. He hadn't touched his food for the last two minutes.

"What if Tarleton offered design services to their clients? Instead of a few design packages with two color options for each, buyers would meet with a designer to determine their style and present options tailored to them. You can include a two-hour consultation in the base price or make it an add-on for an additional charge."

"It's more than I can take on, and with Genevieve expecting, she'll have her hands full. But, if we gave it a trial run, you'd be interested in offering to be one of the designers?" Eve speculated.

"I would." Olivia managed to keep her voice level.

"We'll have to give that some thought. When is the wedding?" Eve's abrupt change of subject slowed Olivia's racing heart.

She looked at Bash. "With him deployed and me starting the new job, we haven't made plans yet."

"We'll start on that after the cruise." Bash laid a hand over Olivia's.

"It's hard to find the right wedding venue. Genevieve's top choices were booked out well over a year and a half. She finally settled on her third choice. If you plan to get married in the Raleigh area, I can give you some location suggestions and my notes on caterers and florists." Eve's eyes lit up.

"Or you could have the ship's captain marry you," Rick said.

"Um . . ." Olivia sputtered.

"I'm sure they want their family to be there, dear." Eve overrode her husband.

"Yes," Olivia piped in. "My mother and his parents would be devastated not to be included."

Bash nodded. "My grandmother would probably kill me—despite my training."

Rick laughed. "I understand. Just thought it could save you the hassle, stress, and expense of planning a wedding," Rick lowered his voice. "I would have given my daughter $30,000 towards buying a house if she eloped and still come out ahead in many ways. But it was a beautiful wedding." He patted his wife's hand.

Olivia's heart raced in her chest. Claiming to be engaged was one thing. No way were they getting married—even to curry favor with the Tarletons to get her dream job.

Chapter Five

"Wow. You look great in that color." Bash's tongue seemed to fill his mouth. Olivia's sleeveless jade-green dress had a high neckline, but it showed off her long, tan legs. Gold triangular earrings drew his attention to her neck, and a matching pendant hung from a chain and pointed right to her breasts. A dainty gold chain wrapped around her ankle.

He couldn't tell if she blushed or if the pink on her cheeks was from today's sun kissing places *he* wanted to kiss. He headed into the bathroom before acting on those urges.

Spending this much time with Olivia had him falling harder. It was widely asserted that men couldn't have women purely as friends. Lord knows he'd tried with Olivia, but he'd always wanted more. Acting like they were in love had him envisioning a future together that he couldn't shake.

As he dried off after a quick, cold shower, he thought about how it would suck to spend all this time together and return to being friends. He dreamed of having someone to welcome him home from a deployment. Motivation to make it home. Would it be worse to ruin the friendship and lose Olivia from his life permanently?

If that happened, maybe he could quit comparing every woman he dated to her and find someone to settle down with. He was ready to commit. Except he wouldn't settle for any woman. It had to be the right woman.

For better or worse, things wouldn't be the same between them after this trip. That realization sucked the hope he'd clung to for a decade out of his chest, but he wasn't giving up without a fight. He wasn't afraid to die on the battlefield. This might not kill him, but it could leave him wounded and hurting worse than anything he'd endured.

He dressed and shook off the cloud of doom before he emerged from the bathroom. Olivia had undone the braid, and now her dark blonde hair fell in sexy waves over her shoulders.

"You look very handsome."

"I dressed up for my adoring fiancée." He winked at her and put on his shoes.

Jacob and Danny waited outside the restaurant.

"I saw you two sitting with the Tarletons this morning. Aren't you brave?" Jacob said once they were seated.

"Rick wanted to apologize about the mix-up with the shore excursions."

"He wants to keep his new star happy. Do tell, how did you save the company that much money immediately?" Jacob leaned forward in anticipation.

"He hired me away from Hanover Tile, so I had a good idea about the profit margins and how low I could get them. I spent weeks analyzing how much tile went into each house and how much overage there was based on square footage. And I went to the job site, spoke with experienced installers, and watched them work."

"Thorough. A girl willing to get her hands dirty and still looks that good," Jacob said to Bash.

"She's the whole package." Bash draped an arm over the back of her chair and caressed her shoulder. "You should have seen us covered with dirt from the ATV ride." She even made that look sexy.

"I'm glad you found an activity," Danny said. "How was it?"

"It was fun," Olivia said. "The beach they took us to had lots of iguanas, and the snorkeling just off the shore was great."

"Good, good," Jacob said. "How did you get cost down?"

"The biggest expense isn't materials. It's labor, especially with cutting tiles. *That's* where we could save money. Coming from the manufacturing end, I know what resetting machines for a special run costs. However, with the amount of tile a builder the size of Tarleton uses, if we have them cut tiles in half, thirds, or even quarters for our most popular products, it cuts time to install a kitchen backsplash or shower by twenty-five percent. There's also less waste, which saves us one box of tile per install job."

"Brilliant. I'll see if our flooring manufacturer can do the same."

"I agree with the brilliant assessment." Bash smiled proudly at Olivia.

"When we get back, I'll send you notes on what to ask and how I calculated costs."

"You're a sweetheart. After dinner, we're going down to karaoke. You *have* to come."

"Are you going to sing?" Olivia asked.

"Of course he is," Danny answered.

"Then we'll come to support you," Bash said.

Jacob and Danny studied the menu and ordered appetizers and wine then quizzed the server like true foodies. They took pictures of their food and oohed and aahed sampling their Chilean sea bass and a pasta dish with mussels and scallops. Olivia shared bites of her succulent lobster tail and tender filet with Bash. He happily fed her a taste of his sea salt crusted red snapper, wishing it was his lips touching hers.

The setting sun played off the clouds on the horizon and added a romantic vibe to the setting. Olivia was more relaxed than she had been at breakfast. Pretending to be a couple was the most enjoyable mission Bash had ever taken on, but success was not guaranteed. He needed a battle plan to turn the tide in his favor, and with one day down and three left, he had no idea what that plan was.

Chapter Six

AFTER DINNER AND DESSERT, the foursome headed to the bar where a blonde in her fifties sang "I'm Every Woman" like a true pop star as they found a table.

After ordering cocktails, Jacob held the song list out to Olivia.

"I'm merely here in a support capacity. Singing isn't one of my talents." She refused to touch the list.

Bash took it.

"Karaoke isn't about being good. It's about having fun," Jacob insisted.

"He's right. My captain can't carry a tune if his life depended on it, but that doesn't stop him from singing off-key and changing the words. And on a deployment, there are times that you need to laugh and cut loose."

"I do a mean 'How Far I'll Go,' but I'm feeling 'Let it Go' tonight. It gets the crowd involved," Jacob decided.

"You sang Taylor Swift's 'Love Story' at that party in high school," Bash didn't let up on Olivia.

"Only because of underage drinking and peer pressure. How do you remember what song I sang a decade ago?"

"He was already in love with you back then," Jacob surmised.

"I don't think so. The girl he dated at the time sang 'Teenage Dream' to him." Juliana's performance included shaking her ass and blowing kisses to Bash.

"We did not go *all the way* that night. Or ever," Bash added.

Olivia wasn't buying that.

"Juliana came out of the closet in college."

"She's gay?" Olivia said loud enough that the couple in front of them turned to look their way.

"She was, uh, trying to determine that back then."

"Don't worry, you didn't make her gay." Jacob patted Bash's forearm. "It doesn't work that way."

"I wasn't worried." Bash laughed.

Olivia wanted to wring Juliana's neck. Not because she was gay but her crappy timing. Juliana had asked Bash to the winter dance before Olivia worked up her nerve. She'd been in the crushing-on-him phase of their relationship cycle. Their timing had never synced up.

"Jacob's right," Bash went on. "I wanted to be Romeo to your Juliet, though it was your *mom* sending the stay away vibes."

Her mother had probably done more than send stay far, far away vibes based on how many times she warned Olivia that Bash was a player like her father had been and would only break her heart.

"Yet here you are today." Danny waved his hands.

"The best things are worth waiting for." Bash took Olivia's hand and lifted it to his lips.

Olivia stared into his eyes. This fluttering in her stomach wasn't supposed to happen. She broke eye contact to applaud as the blonde curtsied and left the stage.

"You want me to take that for you?" Jacob held out a hand.

Bash passed him the folded scrap of paper.

"What are you going to sing?" Olivia asked.

"You'll see."

She wished she'd peeked to see what he'd written. They had endured two less-than-stellar performances and a decent rendition of "Margaritaville" before Jacob took the stage. When Jacob sang the line from the *Frozen* song about being the queen, Griffith's gruff laugh carried from several tables over. Danny shot an annoyed look his way. At least a dozen others joined her, Bash, and Danny in giving Jacob a standing ovation.

The next performer rapped a song from the musical *Hamilton*.

"Next up, we have Sebastián Cruz," the DJ announced, "doing a duet with his fiancée, Olivia Novak."

"What? No. You didn't."

Bash was already on his feet, smiling as he extended a hand to her.

"I don't even know what we're supposed to sing," she protested. And one alcoholic drink didn't give her the courage to sing in front of other people. He took her hand and pulled her into motion and onto the stage.

"We're singing 'Don't Go Breaking My Heart.' She's singing Elton John's part, and I'm singing Kiki Dee's," he said into the microphone. "You'll do great. Just focus on me."

Olivia glared at him, but his unwavering smile and grip on her hand had her swaying with the familiar music. He pointed to her when words appeared on the monitor. She started a beat too late but got the words out. After a few lines, the lyrics hit her. For so long, she'd feared Bash would break her heart. Instead, he'd picked her up when she was down.

Still, she shouldn't mistake him treating her better than anyone she'd ever dated as any more than him being here as a friend helping her keep her job.

When she repeated the refrain, the look in his eyes matched his words as he assured her he *wouldn't* break her heart. The music faded, and they moved closer. She lifted her face and closed her eyes. His lips met hers. The warmth of his hand on her lower back added sparks to the flames he'd already ignited, and his kisses left her breathless. The applause grew louder, probably because of the kiss more than her singing.

Bash held her hand as they took a bow and didn't release it until they returned to their table.

"You two should do that more often," Jacob said.

"I don't know about that, though it was fun," she admitted, her heart still beating hard enough to feel it.

"I meant the kiss." Jacob fanned himself. "Usually, you two act more like friends." His eyes narrowed in suspicion.

"We try to avoid public displays of affection," Olivia attempted to cover.

"Because you're a mixed-race couple? We get that." Danny touched a finger to Jacob's hand rather than hold it. "Some people act like they're accepting and then comment about queens." Danny jerked his head toward Griffith.

Jacob leaned forward before speaking, "I'm tempted to slip their room steward a twenty to convert their beds to a king for funsies."

"A maid had a divider on her cart this morning. Maybe they already have." Danny snickered.

"The beds *convert*?" Olivia asked.

"All the cruise ship beds are convertible from twins to king, honey. They didn't give you twins, did they?" Jacob asked.

"No." They most certainly had not. "But I'll chip in to bribe the steward if you learn which is Griffith's room."

"Maybe Bash should do some covert surveillance. I bet you could find a way in," Danny said.

"No comment. I don't want to land in the brig." Bash finished off his drink. "This singer's good. I say we end on a high note and slip out."

Olivia nodded. Between kissing Bash and what Jacob said about the beds, her mind bounced around like a ping-pong ball. "Thanks again for treating us to dinner."

"It was our pleasure. Have a great rest of your night." Jacob practically sang the innuendo-filled goodnight.

Griffith and his friend got to their feet as she and Bash exited. She walked faster.

"You two weren't half bad up there," Vance said before they made it more than a few steps out the door.

"Thanks. How was the parasailing?" Bash asked.

"Pretty cool," Vance answered, while Griffith gave an indifferent shrug. "What'd you end up doing?"

"ATV ride through the jungle and snorkeling." Bash's fingers rested on her lower back. "Tomorrow, we're zip lining through the jungle—with no one shooting at us. I hope," he teased.

"You're such a badass," she said for Griffith's benefit, patting Bash's hard, sexy abs. Her nipples tingled and tightened. Heat pooled between her legs. It'd been eight months since she dumped Liam. Well, Liam decided he wasn't that into her *before that* based on his sexts, but being cheated on took a toll on a girl's confidence. Between that and the new job, she hadn't dated since Liam. Now, all the latent attraction for Bash oozed to the surface and threatened to explode.

Griffith and Vance broke off when they reached their

deck, but she and Bash continued down the next flight of stairs.

Bash unlocked their door. Inside, the bedcovers were turned down, and a box of chocolates wrapped with ribbon sat on the bed. She set the box on the desk, untucked the covers, and pulled up the sheet. Straps held twin mattresses together, and a foam bridge piece filled the gap. "Did you know they could connect the beds to form a king?"

He held up both hands. "How would I know? I've never been on a cruise, either. Do you want to separate the beds? Even though I've been a perfect gentleman." He drew out the words and gave a disarming grin.

Last night, he could have easily, even innocently, tried a touch here. A booty bump there. At times today, she'd forgotten this was a fake relationship because it felt so right. "*Almost* perfect." With Bash at her side, she felt safe and protected. Even brave. She looked deep into his eyes. Could she trust him not to break her heart?

"If you keep looking at me like that, I'm going to kiss you," he warned. "I'm not talking about a peck on the cheek or hand. But kiss you the way I've wanted to kiss you for a decade."

A decade? Her heart overrode her mind. "I wish you would."

A slow, uncertain smile spread across his face. "Are you sure?"

She nodded, not trusting her voice. Heat in his gaze and the way he moved drowned out her mother's warnings. What if her mother's past hurts had clouded her ability to see clearly, and she was all wrong about Bash?

One kiss led to another before their lips parted. When his tongue brushed hers, it triggered a craving for more. The kisses got hotter as their bodies sought more contact with each other.

His fingers slid into her hair while his other hand dropped to her ass and molded her against his arousal. This exceeded her memory of those kisses long ago. Better yet, it felt right. Not like kissing a friend. At all.

Bash took his sweet and thorough time. She tugged his shirt upward.

He took hold of her hands and stopped her. "As much as I want this—want you—if we have sex, it will change things. I want it to change things for the better. I won't risk you waking up tomorrow with regrets that we moved too fast. You deserve to be romanced instead of falling into bed after a decade of slow dancing around our attraction."

This wasn't high school, and they weren't under the influence of alcohol this time, but she didn't want regrets either. Which meant she had to get his take on commitment. "I need to know why you haven't had a serious relationship since high school."

"I tried. I couldn't commit to any women I met or dated because things never came close to what I feel for you."

She hadn't expected him to confess to being afraid to commit to one woman and settle down, but she thought he'd blame it on his career and deployments. She had not expected *that* statement. Was it a line he used on women? His words and manner came off as sincere, and she so wanted to believe him.

"After a decade, I don't want this to be a hook-up or vacation fling because we're pretending," he said. "I'm not faking how I feel about you."

She stepped back, too stunned to speak as he waited, vulnerability clear on his face. "I've had feelings for you for most of the past decade too."

"Really? You always have this—this wall up. Blew me off when I tried to tell you how I felt." Bash's eyes reflected hope.

He wasn't wrong. She sighed and sat on the sofa, indicating for him to join her. He angled to face her.

"I'm sorry." Her core tightened as she steeled herself to explain. "You know my dad was never involved in my life?"

"Yeah."

"He disappeared once my mom dropped the we're-having-a-baby bomb on him. He wasn't looking to get married or think he should have to pay child support for eighteen years when he didn't have a say on her keeping me."

"Ouch. I thought they'd divorced."

He covered her hand with his, and she gripped it for strength.

"Mom thought he loved her, but he'd been seeing another girl at the same time. He was using them both. He jaded her outlook and made her overprotective. She knew I liked you back in high school. That you flirted with me even though you were dating somebody else was a huge red flag in her mind."

Bash's mouth pinched. "I should have ended things with Juliana earlier. She was fun, but the romance element wasn't there. I didn't know why then. But you can trust me. I want to spend my life with one woman. The *right* woman. And it's time we give it a shot. The right way. So, we'll share the bed, but no sex tonight."

"Just sleep?" It was reassuring yet disappointing at the same time.

"Not exactly. We are going to make out. I'll cop a feel or two. You can do the same."

They'd certainly waited long enough to get here, but that he was thinking long-term was an assurance Olivia needed. The anticipation of building to a climax and satisfying payoff was also a delicious torture.

Chapter Seven

EVEN THOUGH SLEEP hadn't come easily last night, Bash woke when Olivia stirred. "Good morning, gorgeous."

"Morning." Sleep made her husky reply sexy as hell. "You didn't get up and go for a run?" Her gaze followed her fingertips, which trailed down his chest, stopping when she hit the waistband of his shorts. She bit her lower lip and met his gaze.

"Thought I'd save my energy for other activities." He hadn't caved to temptation last night, and he fought to hold his position even though her throaty chuckle made it hard to keep his hands and mouth off her.

"Are we still doing the excursion or staying on the boat? In our bedroom? In the bed?"

"Are you trying to test me or kill me? Because I promised to romance and woo you before I bedded you."

"Bedded? What century are you from?" She laughed.

"I'm trying not to say something crude—or wimpy to make me turn in my man card."

She chuckled again. "I love how you make me laugh. And we're already in bed."

When she nipped his lip, he nearly lost control. He could

do this. Get through a day or two to show her he wanted more than sex. Three days might be a stretch.

~

AFTER VISITING the Altun Ha Mayan ruins in Belize and a day of adventure, Olivia rode a high—not from conquering the fear of zip-lining thanks to Bash, but from being with him. Today had gone even better than she'd hoped. On the long bus ride to their excursion, she and Bash had talked the entire time. He hadn't pulled out his phone to check emails, or play games, or listen to music. Liam hadn't been that attentive even early in their dating relationship.

With Bash, everything had been easy and fun, maybe because they'd been friends for so long. Today had been different than in the past because of all the handholding, touching, and kissing they'd done. Each of those kisses built her hope and anticipation.

"Let's stop in the market for a drink or ice cream," Bash suggested as they strolled through town, heading back to port.

As they passed a group of young boys playing soccer in a vacant lot, the ball shot in their direction. Bash stuck out his foot to stop it. Several boys raised their hands, vying for him to send it their way. Bash kicked the tattered ball toward a boy standing outside the group. The boy's face lit up, but a bigger player pushed him aside and kicked the ball into play.

The boy's shoulders slumped. He gave Bash a defeated smile as he drifted back to the sidelines.

"You tried." She squeezed Bash's hand.

Inside the market, Bash palmed a soccer ball and tucked it under his arm.

"What do you need—*oh*." His intent dawned on her, but she wanted to see how this played out.

He gave a slight shrug. On another aisle, he grabbed Sharpie markers. They found the ice cream freezer and selected two treats each. After paying, they backtracked to where the soccer game continued. The boy Bash had kicked the ball to sat in the dirt with his elbows propped on his knees and his face resting on his fisted hands.

"*Psst.*" Bash got his attention and motioned to him.

The boy gave a tentative smile and scrambled to his feet and over to them.

She remembered enough Spanish to understand when Bash asked his name. He wrote Javier on the soccer ball with the marker. "*Feliz cumpleaños.*" He extended the ball to the boy.

"*No es mi cumpleaños.*" Javier eyed the ball but didn't reach for it.

She knew cumpleaños was birthday. Whatever Bash said next brought a smile to Javier's face as Bash put the ball in his hands. "Is one of those for him?" Bash indicated the ice cream bars.

"*Sí, y otro para un amigo.*" She hoped she said that right. She let Javier choose two.

The bigger boys had stopped playing and slowly edged closer as Bash continued to speak in fluent Spanish to Javier before giving a farewell wave.

"That was sweet." Olivia handed Bash his ice cream bar and unwrapped hers as they walked away.

"It's no big deal. Seeing him pushed around by his brother brought back memories. I'm tall for being Filipino, but I was always the smallest guy in my class. The athletic kids didn't want me on their team. I could hang back or show them I had something to offer. Now, Javier's got a soccer ball and an extra ice cream bar. I leveled the playing field for him to get a chance to be included."

Most people wouldn't have noticed Javier. Bash not only saw him, he'd analyzed the situation and done something. Nothing huge but still meaningful. Olivia's father hadn't given a dollar more in child support than mandated by the court, but Bash's willingness to do something for a boy he didn't know, and would never see again, spoke to the kind of caring father he would be—something that made him even more attractive.

～

"Olivia! Bash!" Jacob waved and motioned to empty seats at their table the moment they left the buffet line in the dining room.

So much for the romantic dinner for two Bash had envisioned. At least Griffith and Vance were nowhere in sight. With any luck, they hadn't made it back before the ship left port.

"Don't you two look radiant. How was today's adventure?" Jacob asked as Bash pushed in Olivia's chair.

"The tour of the ruins was interesting. And the zip line adventure was a blast," Olivia said.

"She enjoyed it *after* she did the first one," Bash clarified.

"I had to go before he pushed me." Olivia nudged him with her shoulder.

"I'd never make you do anything you didn't want to. And I'd never put your life in danger." Which is why he had triple-checked her harness. For all he knew, the staffer might have started working there yesterday.

"You should come dancing with us later. Or do you have plans?" Jacob raised his eyebrows.

Olivia gave Bash a smile full of promise.

"I don't think they're doing karaoke again tonight," he answered.

Based on Jacob's inability to suppress a smile, he wasn't buying Bash's innocent act.

After dinner and enjoying another sunset, they headed to the club, where they danced to at least a dozen songs. When the DJ played Alanis Morissette's song, "Head Over Feet," Bash pulled Olivia back to the dance floor and held her close. Their bodies connected at their hands and thighs. Her chest pressed against his. His hand moved lower on her back, his fingers brushing the curve of the ass he'd dreamed of touching for so, so long. Tonight, he wasn't dreaming. It was Olivia's mouth that rose invitingly. Her silky lips that met his. Her addictive, sweet taste when his tongue touched hers.

She sang the chorus to him. He hoped he had won her over and that she was falling in love. As the last notes faded, she met his gaze. "Let's go back to the room." Her blue eyes were dilated, and her breathing was labored.

He gripped her hand and headed to the elevator. The wall keeping him in the friend zone had imploded, and their fake engagement was about to get even more real.

Chapter Eight

LIKE A VOLCANO that had been dormant for a decade, Olivia was ready to blow. Neither said a word as they exited the elevator and entered their room. Bash ushered her in and locked the door.

This was about to happen. She braced one hand against the closet to slip off one sandal, then the other. "Will you unzip me?"

Bash swallowed, his head nodding. "I'd be happy to."

She turned to give her back to him. His fingers grazed her skin as he pulled the zipper down with agonizing slowness. His breath stirred her hair before he pressed tantalizing kisses to the side of her neck.

He moved the fabric but didn't slide her dress off her shoulders. Not yet. "This okay?"

"Yes." If he didn't take her dress off, she was. In *three, two* —It glided down her body to the floor.

"A thong?"

She took Bash's satisfied rumble as approval.

His hands skimmed over her hips, and his thumbs caressed the bare skin of her ass before sliding to her stomach, then slowly upward until each palm cupped a breast. He squeezed her breasts and rubbed her nipples. His body flush with hers, he rotated his hips so that his erection pressed enticingly against her.

"I want you so damn much." His voice was low and raw.

"Good. You need to lose your clothes," she ordered.

Like a good soldier, Bash followed orders. He managed to strip off his shirt while removing his shoes. After he tossed his shirt onto the nearby chair, he pulled condoms from his pants pocket, then removed his pants and boxer briefs at the same time.

Completely naked, his body was a sight to behold. Lean and muscled. His erection stood at attention, as ready for this as she was.

Their bodies meshed everywhere they could. Kisses grew hotter than the ones they shared on the dance floor.

Bash sank onto the end of the bed. Pulling her to him, he kissed one breast, then the other. His tongue swirled over the sensitive nipple before biting with the perfect amount of pressure so pleasure eclipsed the twinge of pain. His left hand rested at the small of her back while his other skimmed under the fabric of her thong to gently stroke her. He dipped a finger inside and his thumb swiped over its target, sending waves of bliss through her body.

She gripped his shoulders and moaned with need as she rocked against his hand. Again and again. She whimpered in protest when his hand eased out from between her legs.

He stood, slid both hands around the back of her legs, and easily lifted her. She realized things would only get better as she wrapped her legs around his waist. He backed her against the wall, kissing her senseless before he eased into her. Like he instinctively knew this was her fantasy and had every intention and all the strength required to fulfill it, he pressed into her harder and faster. She cried out and watched his face as they climaxed together. It was the sexiest thing ever.

~

"IF YOU DON'T WAKE up, we'll miss our excursion." Bash's voice interrupted her dreams. Only it wasn't a dream.

"I can deal with that." She pressed her backside more firmly against his erection.

"Today is the animal sanctuary. Besides, I need to get more condoms."

"I'm sure they sell those on the ship." She would not repeat her mother's mistake of getting pregnant out of wedlock, especially since she had a shot at transitioning to doing design work for Tarleton. "Oh, but the Tarleton's are going to be there, so we need to go on that excursion."

That got them out of bed in time to make the shuttle to the animal sanctuary. They followed the Tarletons to the sloth enclosure. After Olivia's turn holding a juvenile sloth while Bash took pictures, she handed him the creature. An image of him holding a baby flashed through her mind. She hadn't shaken the image before they moved on to the aviary housing several brightly colored macaws.

They headed to a clearing where a sanctuary employee gave them information on interacting with the monkeys. The woman beside Olivia cooed when a white-faced capuchin climbed up the employee to sit on his shoulder.

In minutes, the dozen or so monkeys in their midst swarmed the tourists, leaping from person to person. One jumped from Bash onto Olivia's shoulder. Its tail wrapped around her neck.

"You don't look like you're enjoying this." Bash tried as hard not to laugh as she tried not to panic.

"They're about as adorable as the flying monkeys in *The Wizard of Oz*."

"They are kinda creepy," he agreed. "Whose idea was this?"

"Not mine. Hey!" Olivia batted the creature's hand from her breast as a woman shrieked.

"Get it off me!" Eve Tarleton's arms flailed.

Rick tried to grab the monkey off his wife's head. The frightened animal bared its teeth and wouldn't release its grip on Eve's hair. Its other hand covered Eve's face, one finger in her nostril.

Bash held out a piece of fruit and moved closer until the monkey leaped to him.

Eve backed away, brushing her disheveled hair from her face. "Thank you."

Bash deposited the monkey on the ground and ducked as one flew through the air.

"I'm sorry, honey. I thought you'd enjoy this since you love animals," Rick said as the group retreated down the path.

"I love *cuddly* animals. Not those." Eve shuddered and sat at one of the cantina tables.

"Can I get you anything?" Rick asked.

"A cold drink. Preferably with alcohol. He saved me"—she motioned to Bash—"so pay for their drinks." She gave a relieved sigh as the men went to order. "Your fiancé is my hero."

"Mine too." Olivia saw his protective nature emerging again and again.

"I've been thinking over your idea about offering home-buyers design services."

Olivia smiled while giving Eve her rapt attention.

"We'd like to give it a trial run in one of our upcoming

development projects in either Atlanta or northern Virginia. However, you'll be busy planning your wedding—"

"We're not planning a big wedding," Olivia interrupted. Despite last night, and them officially dating, it was way too soon to be thinking about marriage. "Immediate family and a few friends. We prefer to put our effort into the marriage." She defaulted to more lies.

"I understand, and that time together at the beginning of your marriage is *so* important. Is Sebastián planning to stay in the Army?"

"He is." As far as Olivia knew.

"I guess he can't relocate at will. I don't see how it would work for you to be onsite with either development."

No. No. No. This couldn't be happening. "I could do initial consults online, and we could commute. We'll find a way to make it work."

"In my first marriage, we traveled for our jobs and spent a lot of time apart. Weekends were always fun, but we didn't build a strong foundation. When we had our son, I changed roles, but my husband was away most of the week. Eventually, things crumbled. You two have something special, but a marriage takes work and commitment. Now wouldn't be the time to have you involved in starting this up."

Then when would? Olivia swallowed as her boyfriend of less than two days walked back to the table with her boss.

She saw her chance for her dream career *and* a future with Bash slip from her grasp. If given a choice to save her job or their friendship, which would she choose?

Chapter Nine

THE HAUNTED LOOK on Olivia's face before Bash and her boss rejoined the women at the table had been Bash's first clue something was wrong. Things had been off while they got their gear to snorkel, but there'd been too many people around to talk.

"Tell me what's wrong," he requested while they lay in the sun to dry off.

She checked, and though no one was around, she still lowered her voice as she told him what Eve had said. "To get the job, I had to pretend to be engaged, and now they're saying because I'm getting married, I'm not a good fit for the idea I proposed. Only I'm not getting married, but I can't tell them that." Her voice broke, and she sniffed back tears. "If I were a man, my relationship status wouldn't have been an issue either time."

"True. But I'm glad you're not a man." He'd expected the change in their relationship to also change the break-up-after-the-cruise plan so they could see where things went between them. This threw a monkey wrench into the works.

"I'm trying to think of some way to convince Eve to let me

implement a trial program. Maybe if I draw up a business plan."

"So, if you weren't engaged"—the tightness in his chest made it a struggle to breathe—"they'd have you start this design program that you want?"

"There's no guarantee, but . . ."

Only the guarantee the Tarletons *wouldn't* give her the opportunity if they thought she was getting married. "But you'd have a better shot?"

"Well, yeah, but . . . Are you saying we should break up?"

"It's not like we're really engaged. That was the plan from the get-go." But so not what he wanted. He held his breath, praying she'd say she wanted him more than this opportunity and could pursue her dream another way.

"You're right. Neither of us expected what happened last night. It's not too late to go back to our plan."

Instead of this finally being the perfect timing for them as a couple, she delivered a kill shot to his long-held dreams.

THEY BARELY SPOKE before leaving the beach or returning to the ship. Olivia's heart shouldn't be breaking, considering their "relationship" hadn't lasted two days. Except it hadn't been a matter of days. It'd taken them a decade to get that perfect day, night, and morning together.

One day for Bash to get her out of his system like her mother had warned her about—over and over. He'd barely blinked when she asked if he suggested they break up. Instead, he reminded her of the plan—one that didn't involve him committing to anything beyond this cruise.

Once they were in their stateroom, Bash turned to her. "Can we, uh, talk about this break-up?"

She couldn't talk about it without losing the composure she was barely clinging to. Begging a guy not to break up with you had never worked that she knew of. Better to salvage her remaining pride. "There's no need. I'll take care of it."

"Oh. Okay."

Sitting in the room with Bash was more than she could handle. "I'm going to get a shower before dinner."

"I'll go get a workout in."

Really? That was it? *I'll get a workout in?* Couldn't he see what this was doing to her? Or didn't he care? She retreated into the bathroom.

Tears she'd held back broke free as soon as the water hit her face. She'd fallen for every line Bash fed her the past two days. He'd gotten a free cruise, and she'd gotten a dose of reality. Her mother had been right.

Could she make it through tomorrow, faking being a happy couple? Why put off the breakup? If they broke up now, she had a shot at leaving the cruise knowing she would head up the new design program for Tarleton Homes. She'd come out ahead if she were over Bash for good, even if she lost him as a friend.

Hell, she might make him sleep on a deck chair tonight. Or tell him to book a flight home from here.

After her shower, she quickly dressed and escaped the room. Wandering around the ship didn't help clear her mind or improve her mood. Hitting the bar for a drink seemed like the way to dull the pain.

"Where's your sweetie?" Jacob sat next to her. She snuffled, and he did a double take. "Oh, honey. Give us two more of these," he said to the bartender. "What's wrong?"

"Nothing." Her voice wavered and not from the rum punch already numbing her brain.

"I was a theater major. You're not that good an actress.

Neither was I. Which is why my parents insisted I double major in something practical like business. You and your swoony fiancé have a tiff?"

He thought she couldn't act? "He's not my fiancé. We're faking it."

"What? Why?"

"Because the Tarleton's wouldn't hire a single female after the Courtney sex-for-sales scandal, so I lied," she slurred the words. "Then I won this trip, and I had to bring my *fiancé.*"

"The part about you going to school together is true?"

She sniffed and nodded. "We were friends." That's why his betrayal hurt even more than Liam's cheating. "And now I've ruined everything because we slept together."

"Was the sex that bad?"

"The sex was fantastic. He did this—"

"I don't need details." Jacob moved the nearly empty rum punch out of reach and signaled the bartender. "Cancel those drinks. Bring her a coffee."

"Bash is a player. And a commima . . . *commimet*-phobe." She couldn't pronounce the word. "When I told him she wouldn't give me the job—"

"She who?"

"Eve. She thinks we're getting married and can't move to start a design division. But it was *my* idea." She poked her finger in her chest as she tried to explain. "Ouch."

"I think I'm following you." Jacob made her sip the coffee. "What happened when you told him?"

"He said we aren't engaged and should go back to the break-up plan." Her mind was getting fuzzier. "So, we're done. Over. Finished."

"Honey, I think you've got it all wrong. He's not going to break your heart like that. You might have broken his."

"What?" How could she have done that?

"You've been together for a hot minute, so he wasn't getting in the way of your dream. But that man is *in love* with you. *You're* his dream. And you didn't pick him."

That sobered her up more than the coffee. What if she were wrong about Bash's reason for suggesting they stick to the plan? That she might lose her job if her bosses found out she lied, made her dizzy and break into a cold sweat. It had been the thing that scared her most—until now. She could lose Bash, who'd always been there for her. That made her chest ache, and her limbs heavy.

There were other jobs out there but only one Sebastián Cruz. What if they were meant to be together? He was worth the risk of losing her job and getting her heart broken.

"What do I do?"

Chapter Ten

"Bash!" It only took a second to see he wasn't in their room.

The ship was still docked. What if he left? *Please, please, please don't be gone.*

She yanked open the closet. His clothes and suitcase were still there. Her lungs worked again. He *hadn't* left. She could make this right.

Where are you? She texted him.

His phone vibrated on the nightstand where it charged. Really? Now, of all times?

She couldn't sit around and wait.

Looking for you. Must talk. I'm sorry!!! Send.

She hurried to the fitness room. No Bash. The track? He wasn't there either. Maybe she'd missed him. Go back to their stateroom or keep searching? He'd text if he saw her messages. He. Would. Not. Leave.

Next, she checked the main dining room and looked among the early arrivals. Then the bars.

Why had she assumed the worst of him? Because of her mother's *good-intentioned* warnings. And Liam. What she wanted had been there the whole time. She just had to trust Bash—and herself.

Where was he? After rechecking the dining room, she sank onto a bench outside to catch her breath and think.

"Olivia, are you all right?"

Olivia raised her head to meet the gazes of Eve and Rick Tarleton. "No. There's something I have to tell you."

As she confessed why she'd worn the ring to her interview and how Bash agreed to pose as her fiancé on the trip, the weight of the lies slipped away. "I was going to say we broke up once I'd proven I could do this job. But I'm tired of faking it," she finished.

The Tarletons looked at one another, silently communicating in the way married couples do before Rick nodded. "You're right. I might not have hired you, but you have proven yourself an asset. I'm certainly not going to fire you."

"Thank you." Olivia nearly cried in relief that she hadn't lost everything.

"As for starting up a design service, we'll have to discuss that more." Rick glanced to her left. "And you two are together or . . . ?"

"We aren't getting married anytime soon." Bash stepped forward from his position a few yards away by the corridor wall.

"Bash!" She surged to her feet and into his arms.

"But we're a couple. I hope." Bash looked into her eyes.

"We'll leave you two to talk. We'll discuss business after vacation." Eve led Rick into the dining room.

"When you said we should stick to the breakup plan, I thought you wanted to . . ."

"No." He put a finger to her lips. "I didn't want you to miss your dream because we faked an engagement. But I want us to be together and see if we can get there for real. Even if we have to do long-distance, we can figure it out."

"I'm sorry I thought you were ditching me. It's just that . . ."

"I understand. I didn't at first and was pissed because I wouldn't think of abandoning you. Ever. But around mile four, it hit me, and I felt like an idiot for not connecting with what you said about your dad. I've been looking all over for you. I meant it when I promised not to break your heart." He plucked a pink lily from the floral arrangement near the dining room entrance. "Will you be my girlfriend for real?"

"Yes." She sniffed back happy tears. "I'm going to take this off." She removed the fake engagement ring. "From here on, I want everything between us to be real. No more faking it."

"I never was."

Epilogue

SIX MONTHS *later*

"Everything was delicious, Mrs. Cruz," Olivia said. The family had all gathered for Lola's birthday celebration, and even Olivia's mom had come.

"I hope you saved room for dessert. Do you like pichi-pichi?" Lola asked Olivia's mother.

"I've never had any, but I'd love to try some," Mom answered.

"First, we'll do presents." Bash stood and helped his mom clear away the dinner plates.

Olivia handed Lola the gift bag with the picture album she'd made.

Lola flipped through the photos and laughed at the photo of Olivia with the monkey on her shoulder.

"I didn't like those monkeys," Olivia explained.

"I love this one." Lola pointed to the picture of Olivia and Bash on the ship at sunset the first night they were a real couple.

"It's my favorite too." She smiled at Bash.

"If you propose to her, maybe you could give me a great-grandbaby for my next birthday." Lola squeezed Olivia's arm.

"Oh, my, um . . ." Olivia's mother raised a hand to her chest and threw a panicked look Olivia's way.

"Lola!" Bash's mom gave Olivia and her mother an apologetic look. "She's old and says whatever she wants. Don't pressure them," she scolded.

"They've waited long enough. We all know they're going to get married," Lola persisted.

"We're not rushing things, so no great-grandchild next year." With how things were going with Bash, Olivia could see it happening down the road.

"Then a wedding." Lola clapped her hands together.

Bash shook his head at his grandmother. "Don't worry, Ms. Novak, I'll get your blessing before I propose."

The first battle for Mom to accept them together had been hard-fought, but Olivia stuck to her guns. Now that Mom saw Bash was nothing like her father, they were nearing a complete victory in winning her over.

In the two months since Olivia started work setting up the design program in Fredericksburg, Virginia, Bash had come up three times. They'd also spent a four-day weekend at Virginia Beach. She'd gone to Fayetteville and attended his unit ball—as his girlfriend this time. Now, even her mom was here to celebrate Lola's birthday as a family.

"I want to go on a cruise for my next birthday. The captain can marry you."

Olivia laughed at how right Bash had been about Lola's agenda. Though the cruise wedding idea had merit. She looked at Bash, who nodded as if considering it too.

Maybe on their next cruise, she would become Mrs. Cruz.

◈

IF YOU ENJOYED **FAKING *it for the Boss***, check out the full-length novels in the sweet-with-some-heat Faking It romantic comedy series. You'll see Cruz again and meet some of his teammates.

And if tastefully steamy, military romantic suspense appeals to your reading tastes, check out the Bad Karma Special Ops series.

Also by Tracy Brody

Sweet with some heat romantic comedies

<u>Faking It Series</u>

Faking it with the Bachelor

Faking it with the Green Beret

Not Faking it with the Colonel

Tastefully steamy romantic suspense

<u>Bad Karma Special Ops Series</u>

Desperate Choices (Prequel Novella)

Deadly Aim

A Shot Worth Taking

In the Wrong Sights

Complicated Past

Free Newsletter Subscriber Exclusive

Undercover Angel

Faking It Series

Sweet (with some heat) Romantic Comedies

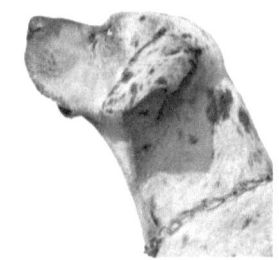

Also by Tracy Brody
Available Now!

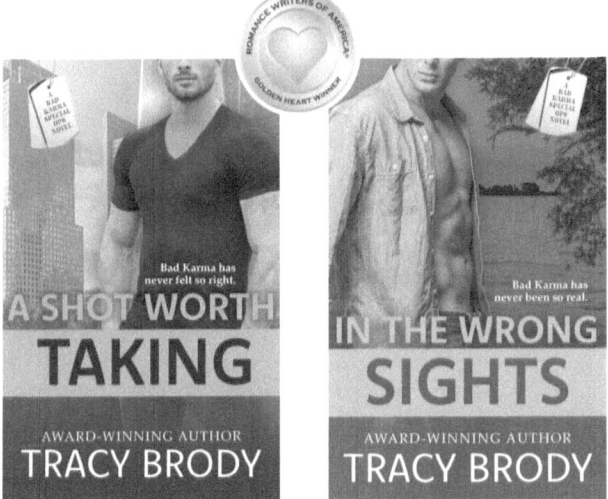

Chapter Eleven

About the Author

Tracy Brody began writing spec movie and TV scripts, however, she switched to using her overactive imagination and sense of humor to write romance books. Her heroes all wear camouflage and her heroines aren't damsels waiting to be saved. She's published four tastefully-steamy romantic suspense books in the Bad Karma Special Ops series and three sweet-with-some-heat romantic comedies in her Faking It series.

Tracy invokes her sense of humor while volunteering at the USO. You may spot her dancing in the grocery store aisles or talking to herself as she plots books and scenes while walking in her neighborhood, the park, or at the beach.

Tracy enjoys hearing from readers. She'd love for you to connect with her.

Tracy Brody newsletter https://www.tracybrody.com/newsletter-signup

Tracy's Private Facebook Reader group: https://www.facebook.com/groups/tracyssfteam

Go to https://linktr.ee/TracyBrody for freebies, music playlist and more.

goodreads.com/TracyBrodyBooks

amazon.com/Tracy-Brody/e/B083G9NHTL

facebook.com/tracybrodyauthor

instagram.com/tracybrodybooks

tiktok.com/@tracybrodybooks

bookbub.com/authors/tracy-brody